Puppy
Pages

With thanks to Heather Ridley and her puppy, Moonseal Pasadena
(Thumbelina); and to A Kid's Guide to the Movies
by Jonathan Clements for movie information.

First published as My Life as a Pup in the United Kingdom in 2003 by
The Chicken House, 2 Palmer Street, Frome, Somerset, BA 11 1DS.

ISBN 0-439-56744-0

12 11 10 9 8 7 6 5 4 3 2   4 5 6 7 8 9/0

Printed in the U.S.A.
First Scholastic printing, March 2004

Designed by Robert Walster

Puppy Pages

Text by Sarah Delmege

Illustrations by Richard Morgan
Photography by Tracy Morgan

SCHOLASTIC INC.
New York Toronto London Auckland Sydney
Mexico City New Delhi Hong Kong Buenos Aires

To all the Poppys of the world.
And all the Charlies too.
xxx

Puppy
Pages

Introducing ME and My Friends

by Poppy

Hi there! I'm Poppy.
I'm a girl puppy. Do you like me? I like you.

Sniff. Sniff. You smell good. Mmmm. You smell friendly. And clean. All soapy and shampooey! Yum, yum.

Lemon shampoo. That's my favorite. That's what Molly smells like. She's my owner.

I love her **LOADS.** Even more than chewy treats AND chopped liver! She's super-great.

THUMP.

THUMP.

She loves me too. She ruffles my fur and pats me. That makes me really happy. **Pat. Pat. Pant. Pant.** Wag. Wag.

AND when she's eating dinner she sneaks me pieces off her plate when she thinks no one is looking. Wag! Wag! She gets in **BIG** trouble when her dad catches her. But she still does it.

Oh, wow! Is she great!

And, **WOW**, am I lucky! Molly adopted me when I was a tiny puppy. She says I was a cute bundle of fur with big brown eyes. She took one look and fell totally in love. And it was the same for me. Wag. Wag.

What happened before then makes me SAD. But I'll tell you because you are my friend....

The lady who took me away from my mommy, brothers, and sisters was horrible to me. She left me all alone, tied to a lamppost. I was terribly **FRIGHTENED.** But then a nice man found me. He took me to the New York City Dogs' Home.

At first I didn't like it there. It was big and noisy and SCARY. Someone took my photo and put me in a cage with this label on the front:

POPPY

Breed: Havanese

Age when arrived: Four weeks

Place found: Tied to a lamppost outside Grand Central Station.

Condition when found: Very hungry. Hadn't been fed for two or three days. Covered in fleas. Otherwise well.

Temperament: Very excitable and extremely friendly. No problem to handle.

Special notes: Good with children. Will have no problem being rehoused.

But then I met **BERNIE**....

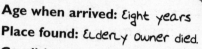

BERNIE

Breed: Bull Mastiff
Age when arrived: Eight years
Place found: Elderly owner died.
Condition when found: Extremely healthy. Obviously well loved and cared for.
Temperament: Can be very sad and often mopes around. Probably missing owner.
Special notes: Bernie is an extremely large dog. This means there could be a problem rehousing him.

Bernie was in the cage next to me. Now he's my best dog friend. I **LOVE** him, even more than doggy chews. **Woof. Woof.**

He looked after me while I was there. He's wise and good. Even when I met Molly, I didn't want to leave him. Molly could see how I felt and she wanted to take **Bernie** home with us too. But Molly's mom and dad said he was so big there just wasn't enough room for him in their house. Now they send him special doggy treats every month so he knows we haven't forgotten him. Molly's mom and dad are **SUPER-GREAT!**

Bernie taught me loads and loads of things. He taught me the *Rules of Doghood.* These rules are

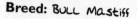

very important. The most important things
EVER.

At eight weeks old, every single dog in the
world becomes an ... um ... er ... what was the
word now? ... Oh, yes ... an **initiated** member
of dogkind. (Wow, oh, wow, what a big word!)

It's very **VERY** important to stick to these
rules. Otherwise every single dog in the
whole wide world *could suffer.*

There are a lot of rules to remember. It took
Bernie AGES to teach them all to me.

Once you've learned all the rules by heart,
you get a certificate. You have to put your
paw print at the bottom to say you've agreed
to all the rules and then bury the certificate
somewhere safe.

Mine is buried under the third tree on the
right in the yard at the New York City Dogs'
Home. **Wag. Wag.**

Because you are my friend I am going to
share the rules with you. But you must never
EVER tell anyone. ...

5

Rules of Doghood

The Rules must never fall into the hands of humans.

I, POPPY, WILL NEVER EVER LET ON THAT DOGS CAN SPEAK AND UNDERSTAND HUMANS FLUENTLY. ANY SUCH ERROR COULD RESULT IN HUMANS DISCOVERING THAT DOGS ARE REALLY MUCH MORE INTELLIGENT THAN THEY GIVE US CREDIT FOR, AND OUR LIVES OF LUXURY AND RELAXATION COULD BE OVER.

I agree to:

1. Only communicate in woofs, pants, whines, and growls whenever any human is within earshot.
2. Pretend to hate cats.
3. Chase and return sticks or any such object that a human chooses to throw, no matter how childish/puppyish, irritating, or pointless the game may seem.
4. Pretend any tricks my owner teaches me are really hard, even though I could do them blindfolded with my paws tied behind my back.
5. Show my owner huge amounts of affection AT ALL TIMES.

I have read and agree to abide by all the above rules.

Signed:

Poppy

I don't know where I'd have been without **Bernie**. He is very clever — but not as clever as **Alfie**. **Alfie** is probably the smartest dog in the world. Sometimes when we were in the Home he used such long words it made my head hurt just listening to him! **Wowzer!**

ALFIE

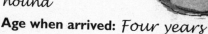

Breed: *Afghan hound*

Age when arrived: *Four years*

Place found: *The reading room of the New York Public Library.*

Condition when found: *Cold and hungry, surrounded by pages torn from books, obviously to keep himself warm.*

Temperament: *Very calm, but irritable around children and cats.*

Special notes: *Alfie is quiet and docile. Would suit elderly owner.*

Alfie was adopted by Professor Pemberton. They are perfect partners, since the professor has **loads** of books. **Alfie** buries his head in them whenever the professor goes out. Boy, does **Alfie** love books. Almost as much as I love Molly. He is one smart dog.

And then there was **MaVis**. She made me laugh.

MaVis

Breed: *Irish water spaniel*
Age when arrived: *10 years*
Place found: *Union Square Farmers' Market.*
Condition when found: *Well fed and well groomed.*
Temperament: *Very intuitive and well behaved.*
Special notes: *Mavis doesn't like being walked. Seems to understand everything you say!*

MaVis is from the Lower East Side. She was adopted by Stella, a fortune-teller. And now they travel around the world with a carnival. Sometimes they work at street fairs. How exciting is that?

Woof. Woof.

And the last dog in our little pack was Tallulah. She lives in Los Angeles now, with a real-life celebrity. Oh, boy, oh, boy. Is she **LUCKY!**

TALLULAH

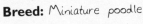

Breed: Miniature poodle

Age when arrived: 15 months

Place found: Sitting outside Bloomingdale's.

Condition when found: Extremely well groomed.

Temperament: Can be standoffish.

Special notes: Tallulah refuses point-blank to walk on any concrete surface and has to be carried on all such occasions.

But don't get me wrong, I'm not the least bit jealous of Tallulah! I'm really lucky myself. **Wag. Wag.**

I now live in Molly's lovely house in the suburbs with her, her mom and dad, and her little brother. His name is Nathan. I LOVE him. He throws sticks for me. And helps me dig for bones and hidden treasure in the yard. Molly's dad scolds him for this. A lot. But we still do it. **Wag. Wag.**

I **LOVE** my house. It's great. There's so much to do! **Wag. Wag.** There's a big fire to doze in front of in the living room. Plus, there's a **huge** garden with loads of flowers to dig up. And I get to bark whenever people walk past.

Woof. Woof.

Then there's **Charlie.** He's Molly's cat. We're great friends. But we pretend to not like each other when Molly, her mom and dad, or Nathan are around. Oh, boy, is **Charlie** funny.

Oh, yeah, baby! I'm as sharp as my claws! Signed, Charlie XX

Charlie uses me as a pillow and sleeps on me. A lot. I like that.

10 Other Things That Make Me Happy

1. My dog bowl. It's shiny. I can carry it in my mouth. And it has **POPPY** written in big letters around the side. **Wag. Wag.** When it's empty, I am sad.

2. Food stealing. This happens when anyone leaves any food out. I get in trouble for this sometimes. **Sigh!**

POPPY

3. Breakfast. Yum, yum.

4. WALKS. I love walks. At
least twice a day. **Wag. Wag.**

5. Playing ball. Chase, chase.
Pant. Pant.

6. Lunch. **Wag. Wag.**
Thump. Thump!

7. Playing fetch. But sometimes
I am naughty and play "don't fetch." This
annoys Molly. **Woof. Woof.**

8. Taking baths. Splash, splash!
I love shaking my fur dry. This makes Molly
scream and giggle.

9. Swimming. I love water. I'm very good.
Even better than Nathan, who has to
wear arm floats.

10. Supper. Mmmmm.
Food. Need I say more?
Thump. Thump!

11

Chapter Two

Dogs are amazing!

by Poppy

Yeah — amazingly stupid!!! Charlie XX

I am curled up on the sofa with Molly, and we are watching TV.

I am VERY comfy. **Mmmmm.** I might sleep now. **Wag. Wag.** Molly ruffles my head, and strokes my ears. I put my paws up and get a tummy rub.

I love Molly. **GREAT HUGE ENORMOUS** amounts. More than any food. Even more than gravy. And boy, do I love gravy. **YUM!**

Charlie jumps on the sofa and sits on my head. I growl. FIERCELY. He winks at me, then hisses, jumps off, and strolls over to the fire. He is funny. Hee-hee.

But I am wide awake now. I open one eye and watch TV with Molly.

Wow, oh, wow, oh, wow! Am I glad I am not asleep! The most interesting TV show in the world is on.

That's a matter of opinion. Charlie XX

It's all about the most amazing creatures in the world. Dogs! **Woof. Woof. Aroof!**

Oh, my. Oh, my. This HAS to be the BEST thing EVER. Even better than peanut butter. There's so much stuff I didn't know.

There were so many interesting, dogtastic facts, it made my head hurt! Here's what the show had to say.

13

Hey, kids...Welcome to another episode of <u>Animal World.</u> This week, it's a dog's life. Yep, that's right, today we'll be giving you the lowdown on "man's best friend." So if you're sitting comfortably and not feeling too ruff (ha-ha!), we'll begin....

FACT 1

Here's your first fascinating fact. Did you know most dogs are able to run at speeds of up to 19 miles per hour? And that the greyhound, the king of canine speedsters, is capable of reaching speeds of up to 40 miles per hour?

> Bet you didn't know that cats can run as fast as 30 miles per hour. No wonder you can never catch me, you old slowpoke!
> Love, Charlie XX

FACT 2

Do you know why a frightened dog puts its tail between its legs? To cover its scent glands. This is the doggy equivalent of you or me hiding our faces whenever we feel scared.

> Yeah, either that or because you're ugly!
> Charlie XX

14

FACT 3

And here's another mind-blowing fact for you: The notion that cats and dogs are natural enemies is overstated, if not totally false. Generally speaking, cats and dogs get along better than cats and cats or dogs and dogs.

That's a matter of opinion! Tee-hee!
Charlie XX

FACT 4

If you're wondering which breeds of dog are the smartest, wonder no more. We've got the answer for you. In order, the most intelligent dogs are:

1) border collie
2) poodle
3) golden retriever

I notice you're not there, Poppy! Why doesn't that surprise me?
Charlie XX

FACT 5

And the least intelligent dog in the world is the Afghan hound. Yep, kids, the good old Afghan is definitely not the sharpest knife in the drawer.

He obviously hasn't met Alfie, eh, Poppy?
Charlie XX

15

FACT 6

The United States and France have the most dogs. In those countries almost one in three families owns a dog. In Germany and Switzerland there is just one dog for every ten families.

Enough about dogs already. What about cats? Charlie XX

FACT 7

Dogs can hear high-pitched sounds (such as the noise some insects make) that humans can't even detect.

FACT 8

If you come across a German shepherd, be careful. This breed of dog bites humans more than any other kind. That's one dog whose bark certainly isn't worse than its bite!

FACT 9

Next time you're moaning that you have to take your dog out for a walk, think about ancient Chinese royalty. They used to carry Pekingese dogs in the sleeves of their royal robes.

That's obviously who Tallulah thinks she's descended from, then.

Charlie XX

FACT 10

I bet you didn't know that there are 701 types of pure-bred dogs!

FACT 11

Did you know that 6 out of 10 dogs own a sweater, winter coat, or raincoat? In fact, most owners have bought their dog some kind of accessory. There are certainly some fashionable dogs out there!

FACT 12

How's this for a weird fact? The bloodhound is the only animal in the world whose evidence can be used in an American court.

FACT 13

If you're a dog owner, make sure you take out your garbage regularly. A dog's sense of smell is about 1,000 times better than a human's.

> So how come you smell so bad, then, Poppy?
> Charlie XX

18

FACT 14

The world's heaviest and longest dog ever recorded was an Old English mastiff named Zorba. He weighed a whopping 344 pounds. That's as much as two grown men! And the smallest dog ever recorded was a tiny Yorkie from Blackburn, England. At two years of age and fully grown, this little dog weighed only four ounces and was the size of a matchbox.

Anyway, kids, that's it for this show. I hope you've enjoyed learning all about dogs and that you'll join us at the same time next week when we'll be entering the weird and wonderful world of elephants. See you then!

Oh, dear, oh, dear. I didn't like the glint in Molly's eye when the announcer said that most dogs own a sweater or coat.

Oh, my, I have a bad feeling. Last time Molly looked like that, she put lots and lots of makeup on Nathan, put his hair in pigtails, and painted his nails pink.

But why do I think the joke's going to be on *me* this time?

Chapter Three

Molly Becomes a Do-It-Yourself Queen

by Poppy

Oh, dear. I was right. As soon as the show was over, Molly rushed upstairs. I went with her, of course. We go EVERY-WHERE together. Although sometimes, like now, I wish we didn't.

Charlie always comes too. He pretends it's because Molly's bed is more comfortable than the armchair downstairs. But I know it's because he can't bear to be left out. **Wag. Wag.**

Molly is hunting through her bookshelves. Finally, she pulls out a book of do-it-yourself activities.

Oh, no. This is what I was dreading. There's a chapter on **Things to Make for Your Pet. . . .**

THINGS TO MAKE FOR YOUR PET

Make sure there is a grown-up to help you with *all* these activities.

ANIMAL PRINT SHOULDER BAG

Keep all of your pet's toys handy in this funky bag.

To have on hand:

- Ruler or tape measure
- Scissors
- 2 pieces of animal-print fabric in 8-inch squares
- Straight pins
- Needle and thread (get a color that matches your fabric)
- Pencil
- 1 yard of wide decorative ribbon
- 16 inches of ribbon with beaded fringe
- An adult to supervise you

What to do:

1. Place the two 8-inch squares of fabric together, print sides facing in. Pin them together along three of the edges.

21

2. Start sewing a half inch down from one corner along the three pinned edges, approximately a quarter inch in from the edge. You may want to draw a  straight line with a pencil to guide you as you sew. Take out the pins as you go. When you reach the end of the third side, tie a strong knot at the end of the stitching. Cut off any extra thread.

3. Leaving the two sewn squares with the print sides in, fold over a half inch of fabric along the unsewn top edges of the bag. Pin these flaps down and sew along their edges as you did in step two. When you reach the end, tie a knot and cut off the extra thread.

4. Decide on the length of your shoulder strap. You can do this by pinning the wide ribbon to the top of the bag and trying it on to see where the bag falls when you wear it.

5. When you've got the right length, cut the ribbon about an inch longer than you want it to be. Fold over a half inch at one end of the ribbon. Pin this end inside one side of the bag, centering it over the seam. Sew across the ribbon twice and tie it off with a knot. Repeat this step with the other end of the ribbon. Make sure the ribbon is not twisted before you start sewing, and make sure both ends of the ribbon are sewn directly across from each other so that your strap will fall evenly.

6. Turn the bag right side out.

7. Take one edge of the beaded fringe ribbon and place it along the bottom edge of the finished bag. Pin the entire length of the ribbon along the bottom edge. Using a running stitch, sew along the center of the ribbon until the entire bottom is covered. Be sure to take out the pins as you sew. Knot the thread and cut off the extra.

8. Congratulate yourself on making this fabulous fashion accessory!

Note: If you don't want to sew this bag, you can use fabric glue along all the edges that require stitching. This includes the seams of the bag, the ribbon handle, and the beaded fringe along the bottom.

DYNAMIC COLLAR

Your dog will look dashing in this designer collar — designed by you!

To have on hand:

•Nylon dog collar •Ribbons (same width as the collar) •Tape measure or ruler •Hook-and-loop fastener tape with peel-and-stick backing •Scissors •Clear nail polish •A nail or other sharp object •An adult to supervise you

What to do:

1. Measure the collar from end to end. Cut a piece of ribbon 3 inches longer than your measurement and apply clear nail polish to the ends to keep them from unraveling. Allow to dry.

2. Hook-and-loop tape comes in strips, one for the "hook" side and one for the "loop" side. Cut small pieces of the tape to match the width of your collar.

3. Stick one of the "loop" pieces about an inch in from the buckle and another about an inch in from the end. Add "loop" pieces every 3 to 4 inches in between on the smooth side of the collar.

4. Turn the collar over and put one "loop" piece about 2 to 3 inches in from the end of the collar, then turn the collar back over.

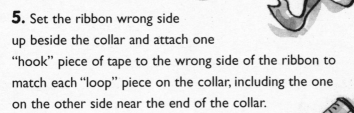

5. Set the ribbon wrong side up beside the collar and attach one "hook" piece of tape to the wrong side of the ribbon to match each "loop" piece on the collar, including the one on the other side near the end of the collar.

6. Wait a few hours to make sure the hook-and-loop tape is firmly stuck to the collar and ribbon, then attach the ribbon by connecting the hook-and-loop pieces together.

7. Ask an adult to use a nail or another sharp object to poke holes in the ribbon in the spots where the collar has holes. If the holes close up (this happens with some ribbon), cut a

slightly larger hole with scissors and apply clear nail polish around its edges.

LUXURY FUR-LINED DOG BED

Every dog loves to nap and your dog will adore this comfy bed.

To have on hand:

•48 x 24 inches of fake fur •16 x 24 inches of any other thick fabric •Scissors •Large needle and thread •Old bath towel •Pins •Marker •A 12- to 16-inch round foam circle (for the bed's base) •An adult to supervise you

Note: If you have a large dog, you'll need more fabric and a bigger foam circle.

What to do:

1. Using the marker, draw around the foam circle at one end of each piece of fabric. Now cut out the two circles, leaving an extra inch all around for a hem.

2. Pin the circles together, fur side facing in, and then sew all around, leaving a 6-inch gap. Take out the pins as you sew.

3. Turn the circles inside out so the fur is showing. Stuff the foam circle inside and sew up the gap. This is the bed's base.

4. From the remaining fur fabric, cut two 30 x 6 inch rectangles. Sew them together at one short end and fold lengthwise, fur side facing in. Sew along the length and turn right side out, so you have a long 60 x 6 inch furry tube. This will form the sides of your dog bed.

5. Fold the towel until it fits snugly inside the tube.

6. Wrap the tube around the circular pillow so there are no gaps. Then pin and sew the edges together. Remove the pins as you go.

7. Sew the pillow and the sides together to finish off the bed!

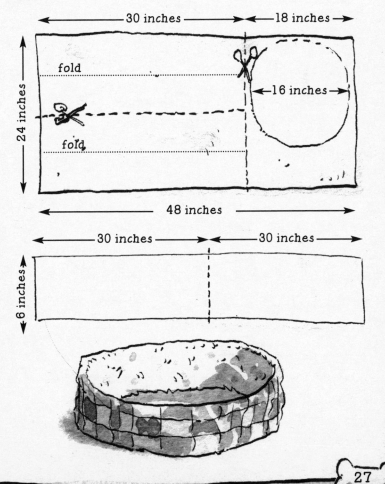

Charlie and I hide under the bed and try not to catch Molly's eye while she reads through her book.

She decides on the dog bed and starts gathering the materials. **Phew, oh, phew!** Molly works so hard that she doesn't even realize it's lunchtime. Her mom has to call her. TWICE!!

Meanwhile, I am practically fainting from hunger. I haven't eaten anything for at least an hour! I try eating a few of the shiny buttons in Molly's sewing box. They taste all plasticky and horrible. I spit them out.

DOUBLE YUCK!!

The funniest part of all this, though, is that Molly told me she is going to ask her grandma to knit Charlie a sweater. **Hee-hee.** I can't wait to see his face when she makes him wear it. The thought makes me laugh so much I fall off the bed.

Woof. Woof! Woof.

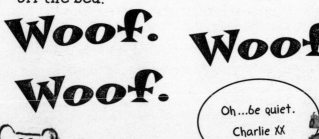

Oh...be quiet.
Charlie XX

Chapter Four

My Date With Destiny

by Poppy

Molly says we are going **to walk** to the carnival! **I LOVE** walks! They are great!

Thump! Thump!

Molly puts on my leash and then we are OUTSIDE! I am happy. **Wag. Wag.**

We walk across the park. There is a puddle. Hurray, **I love** puddles! Jump! Splash! Shake. Shake. BIG shake! Molly is annoyed. Oops!

The carnival is so exciting! Maybe I'll be able to see **MaVIS** in the fortune-teller booth. **Hooray.**

Ooh, I can smell food. Lots and lots and lots of food. **Yum, yum!** Molly wants to go on the rides. But they look SCARY to me! Molly tells me to sit. Sitting is boring. I can smell food. Mouthwatering, delicious food!
My tummy is making noises. It sounds like **Bernie** when he is angry. **Grrr, grrr.**

I sniff around. There are scraps of food EVERYWHERE! Just dropped on the ground. **Sniff. Sniff.** I don't know where to start.

Hot dogs. **Slurp.**
Cotton candy. **Double slurp.**
Doughnuts. Dribble.
Ice cream. **Gulp.**
And chips!

Now I feel a little sick. **Sigh.**

I can see Molly in the line for one of the rides. It is very, very long. Boring.

It's time for me to explore and see if I can find **MaViS.**

I head into a small tent. **Oh,** it's very dark in here. There are lots of candles. They smell funny. They make me sneeze. **ACHOOO!**

I can see scarves. **Lots** of them. Everywhere! They are on chairs, tables, and hanging from the ceiling. There is a funny smell. **Sniff.** **Sniff.** Friendly, but musky. I am a bit nervous.

"Tooooniiiiiight the mooooon is in Veeenuuuusss," says a voice.

I look around.

"I said, the mooooon toooniiiiiight is in Veeenuuuusss."

Boy, oh, boy, whose voice is THAT? I sniff and blink through the darkness and the scarves. **Sniff. Sniff.** Blink. Blink.

I can just make out the shape of another dog. She is very elegant and is wearing a scarf tied around her ears. **Hee-hee.** She looks funny. **Wag. Wag.**

31

The funny-dressed dog comes a bit closer. **Sniff. Sniff.** I smell her. I don't believe it. It's **MaViS!** She hasn't recognized me. I think all the perfumed candles and scarves must be playing havoc with her nose. **Wag. Wag. MaViS** starts to speak again.

"Helloooooooooo! I'm **MaViS**, the Mystic Mutt. I have been trrrained to use my psyyychic powers and read the staaaars by Stellaaaaa the foooortune-teller. She's taaaaaaaught me everything! I can tell yoooooooou ANYTHING yoooooooou want toooo knoooooow."

I can't stand it anymore. **MaViS'S** new voice is very annoying.

"Er, **MaViS**, it's me, **Poppy**."

MaViS sniffs through the darkness, coming so close her whiskers tickle my nose. Then she sits back happily on her haunches.

"**Wow**, if it isn't little **Poppy**. Who would have thought I'd find you here?

How did you recognize me?"

I scratch behind my ear to hide my smile.
"Er, why were you talking in that voice,
MaVis?"

"It's good for business, dear. Since Stella
adopted me, I've learned everything there is
to know about astrology. Problem is, no dog
takes me seriously if I talk in my normal
voice, so I came up with the idea of **MyStic
Mutt.**"

MaVis winks at me. "Of course, remembering
to talk in my maaarvellooous mystic voice is a
pain in the neck sometimes."

 I **love MaVis.** She hasn't changed at
all. **Wag. Wag.**

MaVis wasn't joking when she told me she's
learned loads about astrology. **Wowzer!**
Are star signs interesting! **MaVis** has
written it all down and hopes to have it
published one day. She's given me the first
draft to read.

Mystic Mutt's Star Signs for Canines

Aries

March 21 to April 20

Favorite Place: The local park

Favorite Food: Sausages

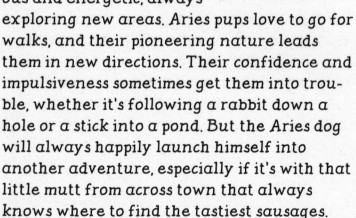

The Aries dog is adventurous and energetic, always exploring new areas. Aries pups love to go for walks, and their pioneering nature leads them in new directions. Their confidence and impulsiveness sometimes get them into trouble, whether it's following a rabbit down a hole or a stick into a pond. But the Aries dog will always happily launch himself into another adventure, especially if it's with that little mutt from across town that always knows where to find the tastiest sausages.

Best Owners: Pisces, Capricorn

Taurus

April 21 to May 20

Favorite Place:
Dozing in front of
the fire

Favorite Food:
Anything rabbit-
flavored

Taurus dogs are loving and cuddly. They are
also patient and reliable, happily putting up
with their owner's habits and strange ways.
The Taurus dog loves nothing better than
spending time one-on-one with his owner and
can be very jealous of anyone who dares to
interrupt that special time. But mostly,
Taurus dogs are quiet and peaceful and like
everything around them to be happy and
secure.

Best Owners: Capricorn, Aries

Gemini

May 21 to June 21

Favorite Place:
The yard

Favorite Food: Liver

Gemini dogs are very lively and are happy
practically anywhere doing anything.
The Gemini dog loves sharing things with his
owner, especially things he's found — like an
old boot he's dug up in the yard. No matter
how old they are, Gemini dogs are always
youthful and have a great sense of humor.
They also have a bit of a mischievous streak,
and they find splashing their owners with
water when they get out of the bath or
burying car keys in the garden very funny
indeed.

Best Owners: Aquarius, Libra

Cancer

June 22 to July 22

Favorite Place: Curled up in their bed

Favorite Food: Gravy

Cancer dogs are protective and caring. They are very emotional and perceptive — they know what's on their owner's mind even before the owner does. Cancer dogs are sensitive and tender. They're also the most sympathetic of all dogs, understanding instinctively what their owners feel.

Best Owners: Pisces, Taurus, Capricorn

Leo

July 23 to August 22

Favorite Place: Anywhere that involves walks

Favorite Food: Bones

Leo dogs are strong and faithful. They are energetic and enthusiastic, and they throw themselves into every activity, whether it's running through a field or fetching a ball.

Leo dogs think that they are masters of all they survey and always act like the boss. Above all, Leo dogs are loyal to their owners — until they spot a squirrel.

Best Owners: Virgo, Pisces, Aries

Virgo

August 23 to September 22

Favorite Place: Their basket

Favorite Food: Doggy treats

Virgo dogs are modest and a little shy. While they know they are the best-looking dogs in the neighborhood, they hate showing off.

38

Virgo dogs are also reliable and obedient. Given a task, they carry it out fully and faithfully but turn bashful whenever praised (unless there are doggy treats being offered). Virgo dogs are happiest lying in the sun, watching their family play.

Best Owners: Leo, Libra, Taurus

Libra

September 23 to October 23

Favorite Place:
The living room

Favorite Food:
Peanut butter

Libra dogs are easygoing and sociable. They are extremely relaxed and feel at home with just their owner or in the middle of a party. The most important thing for Libra dogs is to be out and about among people and other dogs. Libra dogs are laid-back and happy. Not much excites them — unless you count pork chops.

Best Owners: Leo, Sagittarius, Gemini

Scorpio

October 24 to November 21

Favorite Place: Looking out the window

Favorite Food: Bacon

Scorpio dogs are determined and focused, always accomplishing whatever they set their minds to. They are also passionate and forceful dogs, relishing every activity, and they often have so much fun that they end up lying on the floor panting with exhaustion. They can be very intense and have been known to stare at squirrels through the window for hours at a time. Unless it's dinnertime, of course.

Best Owners: Capricorn, Sagittarius

Sagittarius

November 22 to December 21

Favorite Place: Anywhere outside

Favorite Food: Cake

Sagittarius dogs are carefree and freedom-loving. They love wide-open spaces and can't wait to explore them. They are good-natured dogs who love to romp and play with their owners. Sagittarius dogs never hide how they feel because they are always happy and fun-loving.

Best Owners: Capricorn, Aquarius

Capricorn

December 22 to January 19

Favorite Place: The kitchen

Favorite Food: Anything gourmet

Capricorn dogs are patient and careful. They believe that good things come to dogs who wait, so they are content to sit quietly by their owner's feet at mealtimes.

They are very particular dogs, sleeping in a certain place, with the same toys night after night. Capricorn dogs are disciplined, except when it comes to looking for leftovers.

Best Owners: Taurus, Scorpio, Cancer

Aquarius

January 20 to February 18

Favorite Place: Lazing in the sun

Favorite Food: Turkey

Aquarius dogs are friendly and loyal. They stick by their owner's side while watching TV, or lie under their owner's deck chair while sunbathing. Aquarius dogs can also be independent and inventive, often surprising their owners with new tricks. The Aquarius dog is a true friend in every sense — unless his owner should forget supper.

Best Owners: Sagittarius, Libra, Gemini

Pisces

February 19 to March 20

Favorite Place: The car

Favorite Food: Ham

Pisces dogs are kind and loving. They have a giving nature and are very caring. They make great rescue dogs and love nothing better than long drives in the car. Because of their unselfish nature, they are easygoing to live with. They are easy to train and love to go for long walks. Especially if those long walks lead to a park.

Best Owners:
Cancer, Scorpio

My star sign is Aries and I have to say, the description does sound an awful lot like me! **Boy, oh, boy.** MaViS is one smart dog. Almost as smart as **Alfie! Woof. Woof.**

Just before Molly and I leave, **MaViS** says something strange to me.

"You know what, darlin', I see much happiness in your future. A big house and lots and lots of pink."

Hee-hee. That **MaViS.** Always kidding around. **Wag. Wag.**

Chapter Five

Tallulah SENDS a LETTEr

I am snoozing in my basket. Molly, Nathan, and their parents have gone to Molly's friend Meenakshi's birthday party.

I **love** Meenakshi! She always brings me yummy doggy treats when she comes over. **Wag. Wag.** But today I have to stay at home. Molly says it isn't a puppy party. **Sigh.**

Charlie is snoring loudly on the sofa. He is a very noisy sleeper. **Wag. Wag.** I feel warm and dozy. **Mmm.** I LOVE snoozing.

I am dreaming of jumping into a swimming pool filled with onion gravy. **Mmmm!** I **LOVE** onion gravy. **Yum. Yum.**

45

Something taps me hard on the nose. **Tap. Tap. Tap.** Ow! That HURTS! I open one eye. **Wowzer!** A pigeon is sitting on the side of my basket!

Hello! Hi there, pigeon! I jump up. The pigeon falls off the basket. **Oops!** Sorry!

Charlie stands up on the sofa. He crouches low like a hunter. He licks his lips. The pigeon looks **scared!** Poor pigeon!

I shake my head. "Bad cat," I tell Charlie. "You cannot eat the pigeon! He is our friend. **Woof. Woof.**" Charlie shrugs and sits back down.

The pigeon blinks. He reaches under his wing with his beak and pulls out a letter.

A letter! **Oh, wow!** I **love** letters! Who's it from?

Sniff. Sniff. Oooh, perfume! Expensive perfume! I'd know that scent anywhere.

TALLULAH!

Boy, oh, boy. Tallulah. She really is one in a million. She is great. And she makes me laugh. A lot. **Wag. Wag.**

After Tallulah left the New York City Dogs' Home, **Bernie** used to tell me Tallulah's story every night. It's a real-life shaggy dog story.

Tallulah's Story

as told by Bernie

From the moment Tallulah turned up at the New York City Dogs' Home, it was clear she was meant for better things. Well, Tallulah certainly thought so, anyway. She refused to walk on any concrete surface, afraid of scratching her delicate little paws. Instead, the staff had to carry her everywhere. She refused to eat unless a staff member had cut up her food into tiny bite-sized pieces. And she was not satisfied until her fur was groomed to a fine sheen and her favorite pink ribbon had been tied in a perfect bow around her neck. Quite honestly, if it were up to me, Tallulah should have been given a sharp nip on her pretty derriere, but everyone else seemed to think she was adorable. And as you know, Poppy, I'm not one to complain.

47

Even Tallulah's cage looked different from the rest of ours. Instead of newspaper, she had pages from *Vogue* and *Vanity Fair* lining her cage. Her litter tray was spotless and even her basket had a Bloomingdale's blanket in it. It was made of the softest material I have ever felt in my life. "Cashmere, sweetie," she told me. "Cashmere. You should try it."

I mean, what would I be doing with cashmere? I ask you. Newspaper is fine by me — much more interesting.

Then one day her whole life changed, when a real-life celebrity walked into the Home looking for a dog to adopt.

Every dog has its day, and that day belonged to Tallulah. She opened her puppy-dog eyes as wide as she could, pranced around her cage on her oh-so-pretty legs, and yipped in what was obviously considered to be a cute and appealing fashion — although it made me feel quite sick!

The celebrity, a former member of one of the world's biggest girl bands, took one look and fell totally and utterly head over heels in love. Tallulah would probably have felt the same, but she was far too busy being in love with herself.

So off she went to live in Greenwich Village, until the singer decided to try her luck in Hollywood and the pair of them boarded a plane and flew off into the sunset. First class all the way, of course. Some folks are lucky! But, as you know, Poppy, I'm not one to complain.

I love that story. It's a real-life fairy tail!!
Hee-hee.

Tallulah has always kept in touch.
She's great like that. **Wag. Wag.**

She is so smart. And RICH! She manages to
persuade passing birds to fly the letters to
New York in return for all the peanuts they
can eat. That's smart, huh? All kinds of birds
turn up. We even had a stork once.

Boy, oh, boy, life with Tallulah as a friend is
so exciting.

I can't wait to read the letter. What does she
say?

Letters are boring. I'd
rather eat the pigeon.
Charlie XX

Ciao, My Darling Poppy,

I am writing this from the luxury of my very own dog chalet made from the finest hand-crafted pine. I am lounging on the most divine dog-size Burberry bed. You would love it, darling. And just outside my door I can see my darling little picnic table, which I can use whenever I feel like dining alfresco. Although most of the time I eat at the table with Kerry, it's important to have the option, don't you think?

Once I've finished writing this, it will be time to get dressed. Of course I have outfits for every occasion. A maid comes in the morning to help me choose the perfect outfit and dress me.

I'm all on my own today. Kerry is off filming at some

tiresome film set. It must be such a bore. But of course she's made sure I've got everything I could possibly need. Nothing's too much trouble where little old me is concerned.

She's left a video playing so I don't get lonely. Doggy videos are all the rage in Los Angeles, you know. It's so sweet. It shows my very own little doggy friend puttering around a garden, playing with toys, and eating lunch. Absolutely adorable. I love it.

Next week, K has to go and promote her latest film in Toronto. Yawn! But there's no need to worry about me — I'm booked at the Ritzy Canine Carriage House Pet Hotel. It's $250 a night, but it's worth every single penny (or dollar, I should say).

Of course I always stay in the Presidential Suite. The staff there are such darlings. They'll go to any lengths to make sure that my stay is an absolute delight. Upon my arrival I am greeted by my own personal chaperon, who shows me around my suite so I

can check everything is to the standard I have come
to expect. Well, I do have a reputation as a celebrity's dog to protect, you know. It's such a relaxing
place — you can have manicures, pedicures, hair-
styling, ear cleaning, and the most heavenly, relaxing
massage sessions. I have my own staff person to
tuck me in at night and to make sure all my gourmet
meals are to my liking. Their Asian chicken stir-fry is
to die for. You'd adore it, sweetie. You really would.
Absolute heaven.

Which, darling, brings me to the point of this letter.
I wanted to get you a little trinket. Money is no
object, sweetie, you know that. Just write me back
and let me know what your heart desires and I will
send it to you.

Oh, fiddlesticks. Darling, I'm going to have to fly.
My cell phone is ringing. You should see it — it's so
tiny and it clips straight onto my collar. Absolutely
adorable. That will be K. She likes to call me and

talk to me on the phone. She worries I'll get lonely puttering around in this little old mansion on my ownsome. So sweet.

I've got to run, my angel. Take care. Millions of kisses.

Write soon.

Tallulah xox

Wowzer! What a life. Isn't she just the luckiest dog in the world?

I feel a little sad, though. I wish I could see Tallulah again.

I must write her a letter back. I know what I would like more than anything else in the world — a good home for **Bernie**.

Wow, oh, wow, oh, wow! I have an idea! If **Bernie** has his own house, maybe his size won't be such a problem. Then, maybe, just maybe, things will work out fine. **Wow, oh, wow!** Tallulah is just the one to help me.

Oh, I can hear Molly running to the front door. Tallulah's life sounds great, but I wouldn't swap my Molly for anything. Not even for the biggest pile of **chewy treats** in the world.

Chapter Six

The Night Charlie and I Watched Movies

by Poppy

Woof! Woof! How excited am I? It's the dead of night. Molly and her family are all upstairs fast asleep. I can hear Molly's dad snoring from here! Snore! Snore! **Tee-hee!** He's so NOISY! Of course, he's not as noisy as **Charlie,** who is munching on his favorite cheese and onion chips in my ear. LOUDLY.

It's pouring outside and there's thunder and lightning!

Crash! Bang!

I don't like it. So **Charlie** and I are going to watch videos so I won't be frightened anymore! **Wag. Wag.**

And even better, I'm going to tell you all about them.

> **Lady and the Tramp**
> I liked this movie. It was good. Lady was very pretty. She was nice. It was good.

Oh, for goodness sake!

It's Charlie here!

I've decided to take over because:

a) Poppy's fallen asleep.

b) And as you can see from what she's written, if she continues on with her review — well, quite frankly, it'll be worthless.

OK. Here goes . . .

Lady and the Tramp

Lady, a well-bred King Charles spaniel (if you like that kind of thing), is displaced by a new arrival in her home (a human baby — ugh!) and blamed when she accidentally knocks over the baby's cradle chasing a tasty fat rat out of the nursery. She runs away and falls in with tough street-mongrel Tramp. On her way home after a magical evening, she is thrown into the dog pound. Her adventures are only just beginning.

The best part is when the shifty Siamese cats sing "We Are Siamese If You Please." Awesome! Skip the ending — it's really sappy (unless you like sappy, of course)!

Charlie Rating: Three cat paws (out of my four)

Cats and Dogs

Now, this is more like it. A movie about world domination by cats! Lou (a beagle) is an inexperienced dog agent who is accidentally assigned to protect a professor working on a serum to cure an allergy to dogs. But evil cat mastermind Mr. Tinkles plans to steal the serum and alter it, creating a virus that will make *everyone* allergic to dogs (his plan rocks!!!) and make cats the rulers of the world. This movie is done with real animals and people and clever animal-tronics.

The best part involves the ninja Siamese cats — they know kung fu and aren't afraid to use it!

Charlie Rating: Four cat paws

Oliver and Company

Oliver the orphaned cat meets a group of stray dogs led by the Artful Dodger. Oliver is adopted by a human

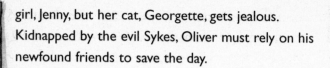

girl, Jenny, but her cat, Georgette, gets jealous. Kidnapped by the evil Sykes, Oliver must rely on his newfound friends to save the day.

The best part is Dodger's musical number "Why Should I Worry?"

Charlie Rating: Two cat paws

101 Dalmatians (animated film)

When human beings Roger and Anita fall in love and get married, their dogs do too! Dalmatians Pongo and Perdita have 15 cute little puppies, but the dogs are stolen by the henchmen of Cruella De Vil, an evil woman who wants a coat made of Dalmatian fur. The dogs rescue their offspring, along with 84 other stolen puppies.

Charlie Rating: Four cat paws

102 Dalmatians (live-action)

After the events of 101 Dalmatians, Cruella De Vil has been cured! Now a dog lover, she is released from prison and takes over a run-down dog sanctuary. But

Cruella doesn't stay good for long — the chimes of Big Ben restore her to her old self. Now she wants 99 Dalmatians to make a coat, and three more for a hood. But Dipstick the dog, one of the original puppies, now with puppies of his own, is determined to stop her . . . with a little human help.

Listen for: Waddlesworth, a stupid parrot who thinks he's a Rottweiler but can translate the language of dogs for humans, and vice-versa.

Charlie Rating: Two cat paws

Beethoven

Canine comedy about a dog-hating dad stuck with a cute little Saint Bernard puppy that soon grows into a giant disaster! Beethoven smashes dishes, bites people, and throws everything into chaos. The dog's already relieved himself on someone before the opening credits have finished — so you know it can only get funnier.

Charlie Rating: Three cat paws

Beethoven's 2nd

Just as funny as the original, except that now Beethoven is a dad.

Watch for: Beethoven pulling the side off a house.

Charlie Rating: Three cat paws

Benji

Benji is a stray dog who lives in a big, deserted house all alone. Each morning he leaves the house, has a chat with a friendly policeman, chases the same cat, and visits the same family for his breakfast, where he is fussed over by two children. When the children are kidnapped and taken to Benji's big house, Benji saves the day. There's even romance for him along the way. Benji is a pretty cool and clever dog, but the movie is *super-sappy* in places.

Charlie Rating: Two cat paws

Babe

OK, so this is about a pig, not a dog. But Babe is a pig who THINKS he's a dog. This is a terrific film — really funny — and it has a great ending where Babe wins the County Sheepdog Trials. There's a fantastically wicked cat too. I could watch this again and again.

Watch for: the little singing mice.

Charlie Rating: Four cat paws

Chapter Seven

Letter from Bernie

by Poppy

Hurray! Hurray! Woof! Woof! Today I got another letter from **Bernie!** Wag! Wag!

I **love** him so much! He's super-duper-pooper-scooper-fan-waggy-tastically **GREAT!**

Thump! Thump!

He manages to send me letters from the New York City Dogs' Home without anyone knowing. Yep, that's how smart he is! Then *I* have to be extra *clever* to get them without being noticed.

Mrs. Pinkett, the lady from the New York City Dogs' Home, comes to check on me to make sure I am being fed. Lots. And that I have a nice bed to sleep in. And that my fur is shiny and my tongue and eyes are brightedy-bright. **Wag. Wag.**

She's very nice. I like her smell. **Sniff. Sniff. Mmmmm.** Friendly. Not as nice as Molly's, though.

The lady bends over and pats me. Pat. Pat. **Pant. Pant.** I like her. She is NICE.

I wag my tail happily and wait till she is talking to Molly's mom and drinking a cup of tea. Then, quiet, oh, so quiet, I creep, creep, creep up to her coat. Very quiet, **sssh!**

I take a quick look around to check that no one's watching. **Phew!** Coast is clear! I bury my nose in her pocket.

Sniff. Sniff. **Mmmmmm.** Gumdrops and peppermints. Don't mind if I do!

Slurp. Slurp. Crunch. Crunch. YUM!

Oops! Wag. Wag. Mustn't forget what I'm looking for. **Woof. Woof.** Here it is! Tucked away in a secret hole in the lining. A special letter. For me! From **Bernie**! Wag. Wag.

Nobody sees me, apart from **Charlie**. But **Charlie** and I have a plan. If anyone does notice me, he is ready to cause a distraction by running up the curtains! Tee-hee! Aren't we smart!

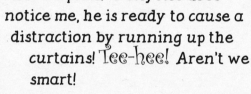

I'll think you'll find that was MY idea, Poppy. Remember, I am smart.

Charlie XX

Quickly I pad over to my basket and drop the letter under my cushion. I **love** my cushion. It has **POPPY** written in big colorful letters across it, just like my bowl. It's great.

I will read the letter later after Molly, her parents, and brother have gone to bed.

Everyone is tucked in bed. I can hear Molly's dad snoring. **SNORE! SNORE! SNOOOOOOOOORE!**

Now I can read **Bernie's** letter. Wag. Wag. I pad into the kitchen and prop open the fridge door with my tail. The fridge light is great to read by.

Dear Poppy,

I hope you are well. I'm fine. I am itching a lot. I think I might have fleas. The cold draft is doing my back no good at all, either. But like I always say, I can't complain.

There is very little to do here now that you have all gone. So I am still reading all the newspapers that line my cage.

Reading all the news stories has made me realize that I am very lucky (if you don't count the fleas and the cold draft). There are a lot of bad things that can happen if you are out in the real world.

Not that I would know — it's been a long time since I've been out there, but I can't complain.

I'm sorry this is just a short note, but I heard Mrs. Pinkett say she is going to visit you shortly, so I have to make sure I am ready to slip this into her pocket without her noticing. I do it when she bends down to pat me on the way out. I hope she scratches me behind my ears — the fleas are biting me particularly badly there, I think.

Take good care of yourself, Poppy.

Best wishes,
Your friend,

Bernie

Poor **Bernie**. I wish someone as nice as Molly would adopt him, so he could be as happy as me. Sigh.

I **LOVE Bernie.** I miss him. Thinking about him makes me sad.

Chapter Eight

Parties and Poems

by Poppy

Wow, oh, wow! This invite has gone up on the fridge — I am SO excited! I love parties!

Please come to Poppy's party.

Come to our house and meet our newest family member!
This Saturday at 2 P.M.

Love,

Molly

I hope there's cake. **Yum!** And bacon!
Double yum! And pizza! **Yowzer!**
I CAN'T wait!! My tummy is growling at
the thought.

Molly's really excited too. She
has asked her mom to write
down all the things she needs
to do for the party. Here's the
list.

Before the Party

1. Write your guest list.

2. Make cute invitations and pass them out to
your friends. Don't forget to include the time,
date, and place where the party is being held.

On the Day of the Party

1. Check that the gate to your yard is closed
and there are no holes in the fence.

2. Have pooper-scoopers
or bags on hand to pick
up any messes when they
happen!

3. Put your Mom's
delicate flowerpots in
the garage.

4. Have enough balls and dog toys available for your puppy so she doesn't start playing with your friends' toys.

During the Party

1. If any presents are opened, throw away all wrapping paper, ribbons, and bows right away so your puppy can't reach them and eat them. She could hurt herself.

2. Think of some fun doggy games, like relay races, hide-and-seek, and hide the treats.

3. Get disposable cameras and give them to your friends so they can have souvenirs of all the fun!

I am SO excited! I want to jump in the mud, roll around, and shake my fur.

Now it's the day of the party.

Ooh, ooh, look! People are arriving! **Ooh, ooh,** they've got presents. And they're all for ME! **Wowzer!**

Ooh, ooh, dog snacks! **Yummy!**

Ooh, a new collar. It's pink and shiny. I love it!

Wow, oh, wow, oh, wow! Doggy treats.

Mmmmm. Slurp.

And a new rubber bone. **Wow!** AND a new rubber ball. Chase. Chase. Pant. **Ooh,** more dog treats.

Oh.

Molly's mom has taken them away. She thinks I've had too many. I am sad now. **Sniff.** But Molly picks me up and cuddles me. She whispers to me not to worry, there will be lots of treats all afternoon. Molly wants us to play games. **Wow, oh, wow!** I am happy again! I love games. We play treasure hunt. Molly's mom and dad have hidden treats in the garden and we have to find them. And the best part is whatever we find we can EAT! **Wow, oh, wow!**

I find lots of doggy treats. Slurp. I feel a bit sick now.

Burp.

Now Molly's mom is putting everyone into teams to play relay games. This is **FUN!** **Run, run. Pant. Pant.** We win! We all get a prize. The girls get bracelets. BORING! I get a sausage. YUM!

I am tired now. I feel very sleepy. I close my eyes and put my head on my paws. I am starting to dream about eating the biggest bone in the world when I am woken by everyone oohing and ahhing. I sit up and **WOW, OH, WOW OH, WOW!**

Molly's mom and dad are carrying the

HUGEST cake I have ever seen. It's almost as big as **Bernie** and that is BIG!

And guess what? It is made of dog food and decorated with bacon and sausages. **Wowzer!**

Triple yum. Slurp. Slurp. Slurp.

Delicious! Molly takes lots of photos of me eating a piece of cake. She says I look cute especially since I now have dog food all around my mouth. **Hee-hee.** She is **FUNNY**.

All too soon, the party is over and all of Molly's friends start to leave, with doggy bags for all their pets. **Pat. Pat. Stroke. Stroke.**

Parties are **awesome**.

Oh, no. Just had a thought. The party has reminded me that it's **Bernie's** birthday next week.

What should I do? What should I give him? Something nice to cheer him up. He'll be all on his own. If only people would see how wonderful he is, rather than how **big** he is.

I feel sad. I miss **Bernie**. Sigh. I wonder whether Tallulah has received my letter. I'm sure she'll be able to help somehow.

Oh, I know! I know! A poem! I'll send Bernie a poem for his birthday. Wag. Wag. Then he'll know how much he means to me!

OK, let me think. Hang on. **Um. Um.** No. It's no good. I can't think of anything. Sigh. It's not fair! I'm never going to be able to write anything!

I've got it! **Woof! Woof! Alfie!** He's superintelligent. Even smarter than Molly, and she got a gold star at school just the other day. Wag. Wag.

As soon as Molly's mom starts cleaning up I'll sneak off. Wag. Wag. It's not very far to **Alfie's**. I'll be back before anyone even notices I've gone. **Hurray!**

Later . . .

Alfie meets me at the door.

He leads me straight into Professor Pemberton's library. **Wow, oh, wow,** what an amazing room. There are books from ceiling to floor. Rows and rows of books. Professor Pemberton must be super-amazingly smart.

"So, **Poppy**," says **Alfie**, "what can I do for you?"

I explain about **Bernie's** birthday and that I want to write a poem but don't know how.

Alfie smiles at me reassuringly. "My dear **Poppy**," he says. "Nothing could be simpler."

Wow, oh, wow! I hope so!

Alfie writes down a few rules first.

Alfie's guide to writing a poem

1. Think of words, any words, that you like or find interesting. If you can't think of any, look in a book or magazine and pick out words you like the look of or just the sound of.

2. When you've written down 10 or 20 words, shuffle them around in any order you like and divide them up into several groups until you get an image, a sound, or an idea that interests you.

3. Take out any words that you don't want and fit in new words including words like *the, but,* and *then.*

4. Once you've gotten that far, it's not too hard to arrange these words to make up a verse or a rhyme or a freestyle non-rhyming poem.

Then we both try writing poems. **Alfie** says I am a natural. I think I am a really good poet, if I do say so myself! **Wag. Wag.**

Here they are! **Look! Look!**

Bones

Bones are great. They taste yummy.
They're just the right size for my tummy.
They can be chewed or licked.
Gnawed, gulped, or picked.
If there were no bones it wouldn't be
funny.

Here's one **Alfie** wrote about me!
I think it's **NICE.**

Poppy

Funny
Understanding
Cheerful
Eats. A Lot.
Licks
Everyone
Silly.

WOW, oh, wow! Cool, huh? Here's the poem
I wrote for **Bernie**. I think it is very good.
Wag. Wag.

My Friend Bernie

Pretty
Awesome
Enormous
Nice
Not naughty
Great big paws
And that's my best friend, Bernie.

I run all the way home from **Alfie's**.
Fast as I can. Run. Run. **Pant. Pant.**

I want to read **Charlie** my poem. He pretends that he thinks poems and flowers and stuff are girly and stupid. But I caught him watching *Lady and the Tramp* with a tear in his eye. He said it was hay fever. But I know better.

Charlie is a big old **SOFTIE** at heart.

In your dreams, buddy!
Charlie XO

When I get home, I can hear everyone in the kitchen. I trot straight in. A letter has arrived about a fund-raising reunion for all the old dogs from the New York City Dogs' Home.

The Home needs to make money. Very, very fast. Otherwise it might have to close. It's an **ENORMOUS** amount of money. So much I can't even imagine it. I tried to picture it in bones. But even then I couldn't do it. **Sigh**.

I am very sad. And worried. What will happen to **Bernie** and all the other dogs if the Home closes? Oh, why, oh, why can't some family as nice as Molly's family adopt **Bernie**?

Molly's dad has told me not to worry. He's said it will all be fine. I wish I could believe him. **Sigh**.

Chapter Nine

REUNION

by Poppy

Molly, her parents, Nathan, and I head into the grounds of the New York City Dogs' Home. As soon as Molly lets me off my leash, I run helter-skelter toward the other dogs.

I am **SO** excited! Everyone is here!

Hi, friends! Hi, everyone! Bernie cuffs me fondly with his huge paw. **Alfie** wags his tail happily.

Just then an excited yapping fills my ears. I turn around as a familiar figure prances delicately toward me.

TALLULAH!!

Oh, wow! I am such a HAPPY dog! We run. We play. We run again. We chase our tails in excitement. I can't believe she's really here.

"Darling, you look wonderful!" Tallulah smiles. "And don't worry, I brought the little present you asked for. It's absolutely super. **Bernie** will love it. You're a sweetie to think of it. And I have a feeling everything is going to turn out just fine."

Tallulah is here with Kerry. They got the invitation to the fund-raiser too.

Oooh. Oooh. And **MaViS** is here. She winks at me from Stella the fortune-teller's side.

I am one happy pup. I **LOVE** my friends. This is better than a peanut butter sandwich with onion gravy and birthday cake on top! **Woof. Woof.**

We run around the grounds happily. It is fun. There is so much to see! There are loads and loads of stalls.

Even better, there's lots and lots to eat!

Hot dogs.

Doughnuts!

Cakes. Slurp, slurp, slurp!

Eventually we all land in an exhausted full-tummy heap on the ground. **Bernie** is still convinced he has fleas and is busy scratching behind his ears.

Tallulah watches him for a while. Then she says, "Why does a dog scratch himself?"

"I don't know." **Alfie** yawns. "Why does a dog scratch himself?"

"Because no one else knows where he itches." Tallulah giggles.

Hee-hee! She's funny. We all roll around on the floor laughing.

"Actually, seeing you, Tallulah, has reminded me of another old joke," says **Alfie**. "What kind of dog likes baths?"

"I know! I know!" I shout. "A shampoodle!"

Thump. Thump.

When Molly's dad's cell phone rings, Tallulah winks at us and asks, "What do you get when you cross a dog and a phone?"

"I don't know," I say.

"A golden receiver, of course." She grins.

I think my tail might fall off as I am laughing so much. **Hee-hee-hee!**

Mavis trots over to see what all the commotion is about. Not one to be outdone, she joins in.

"How do you catch a runaway dog?" she asks.

"No idea." I groan. I am lying on my tummy. It hurts. I have laughed too much. **Ow!**

"Well, hide behind a tree and make a noise like a bone, of course." She smirks.

Hee-hee-hee. I roll over and accidentally bump into **Bernie.** He nudges me playfully out of the way with his nose.

"Come on, **Bernie,** you must know a joke," I say.

He smiles sadly. "I only know one," he sighs. "I bet you've heard it before."

"Come on," says **MaVis.** "Spit it out."

Bernie sighs loudly. "OK, but don't blame me, if it's not funny. How do you stop a dog from smelling?"

"Don't know," we chorus.

"Put a clothespin on its nose."

Hee! I really think my sides might split. I never knew there were so many funny dog jokes!

Tap. Tap. Tap. The lady in charge of the Home is standing on a stage. The rest of the staff are standing behind her.

84

Suddenly, I remember why we are here. I no longer feel like laughing. I feel sick.

The lady starts talking. "Ladies and gentlemen, thank you so much for coming to support us today. I cannot tell you how much we appreciate your efforts on behalf of the New York City Dogs' Home. With your help we have managed to raise a thousand dollars."

Everyone starts clapping and cheering.
Clap. Clap. Clap.

Bernie, MaViS, Alfie, Tallulah, and I all wag our tails as hard as we can.

Wag. Wag.
　　Thump. Thump. Thump.

The lady holds her hands up in the air.

"Sadly, that amount alone is not enough to keep the Home open."

Bernie hides his head in his paws.

The lady holds her hands up again. "But fortunately, we don't have to worry about

85

that, thanks to one very generous dog owner.
Kerry Merringue, who I'm sure you'll all
recognize as a former member of the rock
band Just Girls and now a huge Hollywood
star. Kerry has kindly donated one million
dollars!"

Wowzer! Kerry bounds onto the
stage dressed in a bright pink catsuit to say a
few words. But we're too excited to listen.

Tallulah does a somersault in the air.
Bernie's huge tail leaves a small crater in
the ground he's wagging it so hard.

I chase my tail around and around and
around. Now I am DIZZY!

"All right, sweetie," **MaViS** says, nodding in
the direction of the stage. "I told you pink
would be lucky for you, didn't I? Now all you
need is that big house. And something tells
me that is on its way."

A huge pink truck pulls up outside the Home.
Tallulah smiles at me. "That's your gift."

A man climbs out of the front seat and walks
around to the back of the truck. He seems to

be struggling to pull something out. **Hee-hee-hee.** He looks funny.

A minute later, he's struggling under the weight of the biggest doghouse you have ever seen. **Wow, oh, wow.** It is as big as the shed. **Wow, oh, wow!** Tallulah and I grin at each other. Even I didn't expect it to be this fantastic!

There is a big pink ribbon tied around the middle. Attached to the ribbon is a big label that says:

A big home for the biggest dog with the biggest heart.

With love from
Kerry and Tallulah

Everyone at the Home rushes toward the doghouse in excitement.

Woof. Woof. Woof.

Kerry is still on the stage. She taps the microphone.

"Ladies and gentlemen, when I received the letter from the Home asking for help to keep it open, the least I could do was make a donation. After all, if it wasn't for the Home's good work, I wouldn't have my darling Tallulah.

"So when a second letter came, telling me about **Bernie** and the fact that it's so hard to find him a home because he's so big, I immediately bought the biggest doghouse I could find. I thought to myself, if I can't provide **Bernie** with a home, I CAN provide him with the best house a dog could want. I hope this will mean that some kind family with a large yard will now be able to adopt **Bernie**. If he brings them just a tenth of the happiness my Tallulah has brought me, they'll be a lucky family indeed."

Clap. Clap. Clap. Clap.

Everyone is applauding. And cheering.

Bernie is sitting open-mouthed, staring at his enormous doghouse in disbelief. **Wag. Wag.**

Luckily Kerry is too busy smiling, waving, and signing autographs to take any notice of the lady from the Home who is frantically trying to tell her that she doesn't know anything about the second letter.

Woof. Woof.

Of course she doesn't. It was from me! **Hee-hee.** I faked it and asked Tallulah to find a way of getting Kerry to read it so she would buy **Bernie** a big house to sleep in. Tallulah is so CLEVER. **Wag. Wag.** I knew she'd do it! And the rest, as they say, is history. Boy, oh, boy, I've always wanted to say that.

Later . . .

Alfie and **Mavis** have left. Tallulah is leaving in a bright pink stretch limousine with Kerry. Everyone is staring and staring. What a way to go! **Wag. Wag.**

89

Molly comes over to collect me. I am sad. Even though **Bernie** now has a nice new doghouse to sleep in, I don't want to leave him at the Home. He licks my nose sadly. Sniff.

He slowly starts to walk away. I feel like crying. I am so sad.

But Molly's grinning. She calls **Bernie** back. She bends down and ruffles his fur. "Where are you going, **Bernie?** You've got a nice new home to go to, with a great new family and their little puppy."

Wow, oh, wow, oh, wow! Where, Molly? Where? I hope it's near me. I am so excited. Wag. Wag.

But it gets better. . . .

"Yes, **Bernie**, you're coming home with us," says Molly's dad. "We'd already decided that if the Home had to close, we were going to take you. Even if it was going to be tight. But now that you've got a great big comfortable house of your own to live in, that's even better! We've got a nice big yard for it to go in. Welcome to the family, **Bernie**!"

Molly leans down and hugs him.

THIS IS BETTER THAN DOGGY TREATS!

Woof. Woof.

Chapter Ten

Happy Family

by Poppy

Bernie and I, and Molly, Nathan, and Molly's mom and dad all go out for walks together. It's **SO** great.

When we get to the dog park, Molly lets **Bernie** and me off our leashes. **Bernie's** so excited to be out in the real world. We run. We jump and roll over and over until we land in an exhausted heap. **Pant. Pant.**

Now all my favorite people are under one roof and **Bernie's** part of the family. Things just couldn't be any better.

Not even if you threw in a lifetime supply of doggy treats. **Wag. Wag.**

The End

YOUR VERY OWN PUPPY PAGES

Hi there. I hope you liked my book. To **thank you** for reading it, I've included this part in the back — it's for you to fill in things about your dog, or the dog you really wish you had.

Gotta run. I've got a ball to catch!

My dog's name is/would be:

....

....

His or her breed is/would be:

....

....

94

I chose this dog because:

....

....

....

My dog is/would be special because:

....

....

....

My dog's favorite thing is/would be:

....

....

....

The thing my dog would most like me to make for him/her is:

....

....

....

The thing he/she would like the least is:

....

....

....

My favorite dog joke is:

....

....

....

Here is my dog poem:

....

....

....

....

....

....

....

....

....

....

....

My favorite dog story is:

....

....

....

....

....

....

....

....

....

....

....

Here's a fantastic dog recipe:

....

....

....

....

Other amazing dog facts:

....

....

....

Great party games for pups:

....

....

....

....

My favorite movie about dogs is:
(And here's why I like it)

....

....

....

....

....

....

I give it 🐾 · 🐾 · 🐾 · 🐾 out of four paw prints.

Signed:
....

Would you like to help dogs like Poppy and Bernie?

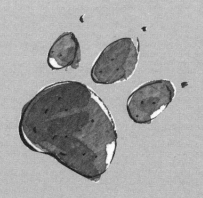

(then turn the page)

Here's where to start....

The American Society for the Prevention of Cruelty to Animals (ASPCA) is a great resource for learning all about how you can help abused, neglected, or abandoned pets. Go to their Web site (*www.aspca.org*) to find out how you can adopt a pet, donate money to shelters and other programs, and much, much more. You can even request a free information packet to be sent to you!

Pets911 is another helpful organization that focuses on what you can do for animals in your own backyard (so to speak!). Log on to their Web site (*www.1888pets 911.org*), where you can search for many pets that are available for adoption, learn about local animal shelters and rescue groups, and find out about various animal events in your community.

If you're specifically interested in how you can help dogs and pups, check out PuppySites.com (*www.puppysites.com/ rescue.html*) to learn all you can about dog shelters in various locations throughout the United States.

Petfinders.org is yet another great Web site that links to animal shelters all over the country!

As you can see, the Internet has a lot of information about animals in need. But you can also always check your local library for books and directories, or ask for information at your neighborhood animal shelter or veterinarian's office.